GLADIATOR BOY
vs
THE GOLEM ARMY

GLADIATOR BOY

Win an exclusive
Gladiator Boy T-shirt and goody bag!

Use the special code below to decode the sentence, then send it in to us.
Each month we will draw one winner to receive a Gladiator Boy T-shirt
and goody bag.

Send your entry on a postcard to:
GLADIATOR BOY: ESCAPE FROM THE EAST COMPETITION,
Hodder Children's Books, 338 Euston Road, London NW1 3BH

Only one entry per child.
Final Draw: 31 December 2010

You can also enter this competition via the Gladiator Boy website
WWW.GLADIATORBOY.COM

GLADIATOR BOY

vs

THE GOLEM ARMY

DAVID GRIMSTONE

Hodder
Children's
Books

A division of Hachette Children's Books

For Gemma Beloni, who managed to sleep despite the swirling vortex under the bed.

This new series is dedicated to Leilani Sparrow, who has worked tirelessly with Gladiator Boy since his arrival. Thanks also to Anne McNeil, who has stood in my corner since day one.

HOW MANY OF
GLADIATOR BOY
SERIES ONE HAVE YOU COLLECTED?

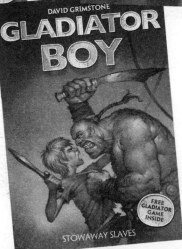

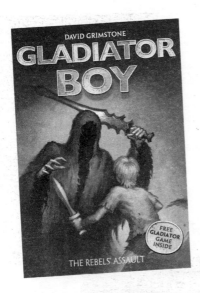

DAVID GRIMSTONE

GLADIATOR
BOY

THE REBELS' ASSAULT

FREE
GLADIATOR
GAME
INSIDE

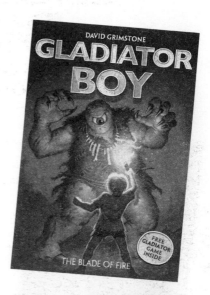

DAVID GRIMSTONE

GLADIATOR
BOY

THE BLADE OF FIRE

FREE
GLADIATOR
GAME
INSIDE

DAVID GRIMSTONE

GLADIATOR
BOY

RESCUE MISSION

FREE
GLADIATOR
GAME
INSIDE

CHINA

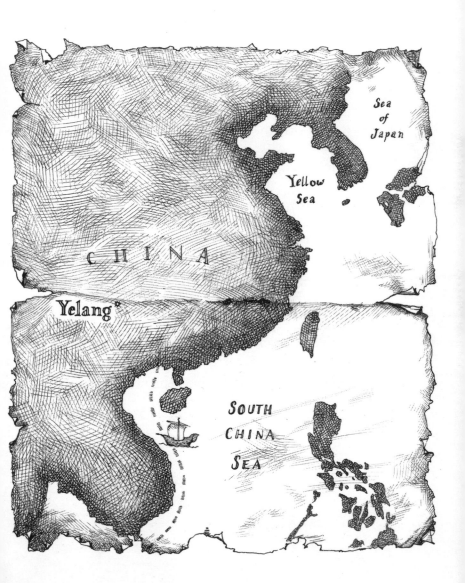

Sea
of
Japan

Yellow
Sea

CHINA

Yelang

SOUTH
CHINA
SEA

PREVIOUSLY IN GLADIATOR BOY

While Slavious Doom holds Gladius, Teo, Argon and Olu as his prisoners, Decimus and Ruma infiltrate the fort on the top of Pin Yon Rock to seek out the legendary White Snake. They soon discover that the fort is full of curious statues, and eventually happen upon the fabled reptile itself. However, during the battle that follows the snake's discovery, Decimus is bitten several times. He destroys the snake but loses consciousness, leaving Ruma alone in a place where – very suddenly – the statues don't seem quite as still as they once were . . .

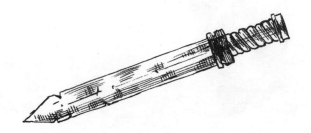

CHAPTER
I

AN ARMY
RISES

Ruma looked on with mounting horror as the statues in the room slowly came to life. His fingers scrambled on the floor for his sword as, one by one, the figures shuffled forward on legs that had been still as stone just a few moments ago. They carried no weapons, but fists like stone hammers swung at their sides, sending off sparks every time they glanced the tree-trunk legs that propelled the creatures onward. The arms looked as though they could crush skulls with the smallest effort.

A sudden glance down at Decimus told Ruma that his friend was in serious trouble: the young gladiator's throat was now tinged with green from the White Snake's poison, and he was rapidly losing consciousness.

Ruma used one hand to drag his friend away from the remains of the bulky snake, while keeping a terrified eye on the advancing statues.

'Stay away!' Ruma held up his sword as the statues approached ever nearer with their fists raised as if to strike him down. He reached down to slap his friend lightly across the face.

'Wake up, Decimus! Wake up! We need to get out of here!' He shook him again, but got no response. Outside, the rising noise of Doom's siege army was clearly audible. The first statue was almost upon them now.

Ruma stepped over his prone friend, swung the sword around in a wild arc and ... gasped in horror as it shattered against the arm of the advancing statue.

Ruma looked down at the broken blade, his

jaw hanging open with surprise. At that same moment a loud and terrible voice exploded in the room like a thunderclap.

The golem army has awoken. All must now prepare to face their doom!

Ruma was frozen to the spot with fear. When the voice spoke again, it was even louder than before … as the figure took several steps forward and snatched him by the throat, hoisting him into the air.

Insignificant human – now you taste death!

The golem hurled Ruma at the alcove which had contained the snake's casket, and he screamed with pain as his body hit the stone. Scrambling to his feet, he tried to make for the far side of the room, but two other golems blocked the door. It was only when they started to speak that Ruma realized their lips were not moving and that no voice was actually audible in the room. Instead, their hateful, booming tones were going directly into his head.

Come this way, little mouse . . . and you will die at OUR hand.

Ruma staggered around in a bewildered state, his body bruised and his bones aching. He cast a pained glance at Decimus, and saw to his relief that the young gladiator was at last beginning to stir. The green tinge was still upon him, but at least he was moving.

Determined to help his friend, Ruma made a desperate lunge for the middle of the room and spun around, trying to face *all* of the creatures at once.

'Come for me, then!' he said aloud. 'I will fight

you with my last breath!'

You will try! Tiny morsel – meet your end!

The golems all charged at once, crossing the room with a terrifying speed that gave Ruma no chance to dodge them. Facing imminent death, the Etrurian closed his eyes and prepared for the impact of the assault. When nothing happened, still flinching, he opened one eye.

The creatures were surrounding him, their fists raised to within an inch of his skull. As Ruma looked on with grim confusion, they slowly began to withdraw.

'What's happening?' the Etrurian gasped. 'You were going to kill me!'

There was no reply to his words, however, and he was left alone in the middle of the room as the golems began to gather around Decimus.

'Leave him alone!' Ruma screamed, looking around frantically for another weapon. 'Come for me! You wanted to kill *me*!'

However, as the young gladiator clambered to his feet on the opposite side of the room, it quickly became clear that Decimus himself was *not* on the menu. A steely, determined look was visible on his face, and the green tinge to the flesh around his throat lent Decimus a new menace.

The young gladiator glanced at each of the golems in turn, then moved through them and stood before Ruma, who was still shaking with confusion.

'Decimus – are you OK? The snake poison—'

'I think I'm fine,' the young gladiator admitted, and Ruma was surprised to see a half-

smile on his friend's face. 'I actually feel
stronger, as if I could run the trials of the arena
all over again! It's as if the snake's venom wasn't
poison at all. It's like an energy potion or
something. It's . . . very strange.'

'These creatures, though – what about them?

They speak inside your head! One second they were charging at me, the next—'

'Yes.' Decimus nodded. 'They spoke to me, too. I have control of them.'

'You – you what?'

Ruma suddenly darted a glance at the golems and followed his gaze back to the point where Decimus was standing, grinning at him.

'What do you mean *you have control of them*? HOW?'

'As soon as I awoke, I could just feel them in my mind, bowing down to me. They say that whoever kills the White Snake has command of their services. THAT is why Doom didn't want me to kill the White Snake: he knew what it would mean for me, for you, for all of us!'

Ruma's trembling hands rubbed at his

forehead as he tried to make sense of what he was hearing.

'B-but,' he managed, his voice even more shaky than his tired body, 'there are loads of them in the fort – they're all over the courtyard. There . . . there must be a hundred or more!'

A sudden gleam flashed in the eyes of Decimus Rex.

'I know,' he growled. 'And, in a few minutes, so will Slavious Doom. We're going to end this once and for all, Ruma – we're going into battle.'

CHAPTER II

WAR ON THE ROCK

S lavious Doom stood on the short, dusty path that led from the base of Pin Yon Rock to the great double doors of the fort. Many of the overlord's men were gathered around him, but he had a distracted, almost vacant look in his eyes.

The army sprawled all over the rock. They had held the fort under siege for what seemed like a lifetime, and many of them had become lazy and fixed in their various daily routines.

One officer approached Doom, who had removed his demon-helmet and cast it on to the rocks in irritation.

'What is your command, my lord?' he said. 'The boys haven't been seen at the window for nearly an hour, now. If they're not going to come out, we have little choice but to wait for—'

'Send word to my ship,' Doom interrupted him, his voice a vile thunder on the rock that caused all of the army to sit up, more aware than ever that their master was among them. 'I want every man, pirate, guard and soldier in my employ here on the rock. More importantly, I want Groach . . . and *all* the remaining slaves.'

When the officer hesitated, Doom slammed his armoured fist into the side of the man's face.

'What are you waiting for? Do it NOW!'

The man flew sideways, crashed to the ground and then scrambled to find his feet once again. Then he dashed off towards the base of the rock, screaming commands at several of the distant rowing boats gathered there.

Decimus strode through the halls of the fort as
if he'd been possessed by the spirit of a great
general. His arms swung at his sides and his feet
slapped the floor with every step. Behind him,
Ruma staggered along, glancing back
occasionally to see more and more of the golems
amassing in their wake.

It was obvious that Decimus was making for
the courtyard and, having come in that way,
Ruma knew just how many golems would be
out there, waiting for them.

'What are you going to do?' he gasped, as his
friend retrieved two swords from a stack beside

one of the
enormous
upturned tables in
the hall they were
travelling through.

'I told you,'
Decimus snapped.
'We're going to march
out on Doom and his men.
I know the sides aren't even,
but from what I've
seen each one of
these golems

could take on three of the enemy . . . and that gives us an edge in battle.'

'B-but what about Groach? He's a monster!'

Decimus stopped and spun on his heels. His throat was now flushed with a brighter hue of green and even his eyes flashed like wet emeralds – it was almost as if the venom had taken hold of him completely.

'Listen to me, Ruma. I feel so strong right now that I would gladly take on Groach, myself. We'll deal with the *monster* when the time comes. Our first job is to take on Doom's army – can you help me to do that or not?'

'I'll try.'

Decimus marched into the courtyard, where lines upon lines of golems awaited his command. Ruma knew the young gladiator was communicating with them telepathically, but had no idea exactly what he was ordering them to do until several of the creatures moved over to the great double doors and began to lift the enormous iron bar that braced the fort against intruders. They raised it up with very little effort, and the two boys covered their ears as it hit the ground with a resounding clang.

The golems immediately formed a marching line behind it.

Decimus put a hand to his head and concentrated, and Ruma stepped back as the golems began to gather into a charging unit. Two of the creatures stayed detached from the rest, one positioned either side of the great doors awaiting the psychic command to heave them open.

Decimus strode across the courtyard to the head

of the amassing golems.

'You ready?' he called to his friend, glancing sideways.

The Etrurian steeled himself, and nodded. 'Then we CHARGE!'

There was a moment of silence following Decimus's cry. Then, slowly, the sentry golems dragged open the towering doors of the fort ... and the army moved forward.

'On your feet! On your FEEEEET!'

Doom's war sergeants yelled their battle cries as the Roman army that had been so relaxed and comfortable in their siege of Pin Yon Rock suddenly came to realize they were under attack.

'Move! Mooooove!'

The troops rallied quickly, seething together in great lines on the rocky path as the horde of clay-like warriors erupted from the fort, with Decimus and Ruma both leading the charge.

Only one face in the mass of startled, frightened soldiers didn't look the least bit surprised.

Slavious Doom stood on top of a granite

outcrop, his hands fastened so tightly

around Olu's neck that he was practically

choking the young slave. Beside him,

Groach cast a

monstrous, hulking shadow over the path nearby. A small group of guards had also joined their master and his terrifying apprentice, and Teo, Gladius and Argon were ensnared in a tight circle of thick ropes.

As the two armies met head on, colliding with terrible ferocity on the rocks, a wave of screaming war cries from the humans echoed all around.

The golems were devastating, slamming into three or four soldiers at a time and sending them all flying off in different directions. One of the creatures had actually picked up a guard by his feet and was using the unfortunate Roman to blast away his fellow soldiers, swinging the man around as if he were waving a stick. In a few places, the golems themselves were being defeated – but it took ten or more men to break down one golem with a series of

well-aimed sword strikes. There could be little doubt that the golems were winning the battle.

Amid the chaos, Decimus Rex and Ruma thundered through lines of soldiers, leaping and dodging clumsy attacks and delivering better placed blows of their own. Ruma catapulted himself over two blades that came to meet him in frenzied swipes, and used his own sword hilt to pummel the wielders both into submission. The scrawny Etrurian was so fast and skilful that he'd dropped the first man before his companion even knew what was going on.

A little way in front of him, Decimus was taking on a group of Doom's veteran war sergeants, matching them all sword for sword and blocking two or three sweeps at a time with little effort. Eventually, he broke the blade held by one man, shattered the helmet worn by another and blinded a third with a kick so hard that the man's body actually went numb for several seconds, and he staggered around in a daze.

The sound of battle raged on Pin Yon Rock. Under the burning sun, tortured screams signalled the death of the human army ...while the golems were destroyed to a sound similar to plates shattering on hard ground.

Still, the soldiers outnumbered their unearthly enemies by a long way ... and the battle looked like it could continue for a considerable time.

Slavious Doom, however, had guessed the outcome.

'We're defeated,' he snarled to his one remaining war sergeant. 'Get two of the boats ready, and have a handful of your men join you. Leave one boat for us, and take the other to the ship. Once you are there, go into my cabin and release the two giant vultures I have caged there. Do you understand these instructions?'

'Y-yes, sir!' the sergeant snapped back. 'Y-you're not coming away right n-now, sir?'

Doom returned his attention to the battle.

'Not yet,' he muttered.

No sooner had the sergeant scurried away to follow his master's instructions, than one of the golems broke free of the battle and raced toward the rock. Moving with remarkable speed for a creature that was basically an animation of crafted mud, it surged into the air and hurtled towards Slavious Doom.

The overlord stood his ground, watching the golem's approach with a grim determination before

reaching for his own great sword. Keeping one
hand tightly around Olu's throat, he quickly lifted
out his weapon and prepared to defend himself.

He needn't have bothered, however, as Groach
stepped in front of him at the last minute and, with
a roaring growl, drove a fist into the middle of the
golem. It erupted out of the golem's back with a
shower of splinters and the
creature fell apart and
crumbled to the
ground.

'Good,'
Doom snarled,
as Olu coughed out
some of the dust
that had been
thrown into

his face during the clash. 'Now we wait.'

The battle continued, but the end was drawing near. There were few golems left, but even fewer soldiers – Doom's army had been completely annihilated by the raging servants of the White Snake.

When the last Roman guard dropped his sword, staggered off clutching his stomach and tumbled from the edge of the rock into the ocean far below, there were only six golems left.

Decimus and Ruma stared around at the wreckage of the battle, their weary expressions betraying the toll it had taken upon them. Then they both looked up to where Slavious Doom was standing, and awaited the evil overlord's next move.

CHAPTER III

AIR ATTACK!

'**D**ECIMUS REX!'

Doom's voice echoed out over the rock, and the remaining golems immediately turned to charge in his direction. However, they quickly stopped and returned to a ready position, as Decimus silently commanded them to halt.

The young gladiator and his companion both looked up at the outcrop on which the grim overlord stood, Olu still clutched in his arms.

'You're beaten, Doom!' Decimus screamed in a wild rage. 'Your army is defeated and whatever chance you had of commanding the golems and taking them with you is gone – I killed the White Snake. If you dreamed of attacking the Empire with these *things* – that dream is over. If you wanted the strength the White Snake's poison has given me, you can't have that either. All your plans are now lost shadows, along with the Blade of Fire and every other pathetic attempt you've made at making yourself MORE than the cowardly wretch that you truly are. Now COME down here and face me in combat – let's finish this once and for ALL.'

Doom's face was a complete picture of hatred, but he forced his mouth into a twisted smile, nonetheless.

'You will *pay* for the damage you have done here, today,' he boomed. 'But first, we will take your friends back to the ship – there, Groach will show them a new meaning of the word "pain".'

Decimus and Ruma shared a confident glance.

'You'll never get off the rock, Doom. If you think *four* guards and that monster standing

beside you will be enough to stop us and our clay *friends* here – you are *gravely* mistaken.'

Doom looked into the air briefly, and allowed himself a smile. Two small, dark specks had appeared in the sky, and were growing larger with every passing second.

Noticing the demonic smile, Decimus followed the overlord's gaze and spotted the birds swooping towards the rock. At first, he took them for two great gulls, but as they twisted through the air and began to drop further and further, it became clear that they were vultures ... and each one was absolutely enormous.

Doom raised his hands in the air, and screamed out a strange and twisted cry.

Decimus drew back immediately, almost crashing into Ruma as he readied his sword and took up a defensive stance.

However, the young gladiator still had his wits about him … and the remaining golems immediately rushed towards the outcrop to defend their captain.

As the six unearthly warriors clambered on to the rocks, Doom hoisted Olu into the air and hurled the thin slave upon them. Then he commanded Groach to attack and beat an immediate retreat, leaping over rocks and sliding down the dusty path towards the boat that had been left for him.

Olu collided with the golems, but was thrown aside at the last minute like a bundle of rags. He hit the dusty path and tumbled head over heels, scraping to a halt at the feet of Ruma, who quickly helped him up.

A wind seemed to whip up out of nowhere, chilling the air.

Groach slammed into the golems who had surrounded him on the outcrop and begun to systematically attackhim with a series of pummelling blows. Groach took each of these in his stride, and began to fight back. Hard. It took him a long time to dismantle *one* golem, however; he'd have his work cut out with six.

The vultures descended upon Decimus in a whirlwind of screeching beaks and scratching claws. His one sword strike missed both creatures,

and he
was quickly
forced to protect
himself with
flailing
punches as the
two crazed
birds flapped
around him in a
wild frenzy.
When one of them
managed to snare his arm, it beat
its shaggy wings with such fury that he actually
felt his feet leave the ground for a second. If the
other one took hold as well, he would be in *dire*
trouble...

Ruma and Olu had made a determined dash

for the back of the rocky outcrop and, clambering up behind Groach and the golems, quickly set to work releasing the others from their bonds. Ruma jammed his sword behind the ropes and began to saw madly at them, Olu helping him with every downward stroke.

'Quicker!' Argon snapped. 'You have to get us out before those THINGS drag Decimus into the sky!'

'You think I'm hanging around, here?' Ruma screamed back at him. 'This rope is thicker than your ARM!'

Groach had destroyed half of the golems by the time Ruma managed to release the others, but the remaining three warriors had the big monster in a pincer movement, and he didn't seem able to get his crushing fingers on one before another caught him off guard from the opposite side. The beast was distracted – for the time being, at least.

Ruma watched the last of the ropes fall away, and then stepped back. To his astonishment, as Argon and Teo began to massage their aching wrists, Gladius immediately took off in the direction of the fort.

'Hey!' Ruma cried, glancing at Argon and Teo but finding that they looked equally puzzled by their friend's actions. 'Where are you going? Gladius! Come back! Gladius!'

There was no stopping him, however – he was evidently set on reaching the fort as quickly as possible. He simply glanced back over his shoulder, screamed, 'No time!' at the top of his voice and disappeared beyond the great doors.

Argon and Olu both turned to Teo, expectantly, and the little slave took the hint and ran off after the retreating shape of Gladius.

Back on the rock, Groach finished demolishing the golems and quickly spun around, his bulbous muscles almost bursting from his flesh with every movement. He let out a grim roar, and then charged at the slaves.

Olu and Ruma dodged aside, but Argon was slower and only managed to move far enough so that Groach just touched him rather than hitting him full in the chest. Even so, the sturdy Gaul was sent crashing to the ground. Giving his prey no time to think, Groach snatched Argon up from the rock and immediately began to throttle him, just like he had done with Gladius in the grounds of the Winter Palace.

Ruma and Olu both leapt into action. Olu took a running jump and landed squarely on the back of the monster, but Groach didn't even seem to notice and the little slave quickly felt like a gnat on an elephant. It was only when he dug his broken fingernails into the giant's back that he got a reaction from him. Still choking

Argon with one hand, Groach twisted his body and slammed an elbow into Olu's chest, sending the little slave flying towards the edge of the cliff . . .

'Olu! Oluuuuuuuu!' cried Ruma.

Olu slid towards the drop in a shower of small stones, but managed to seize hold of a single sprig of weed that, although it snapped after a few seconds in his grip, stopped him from falling to his doom.

Ruma screamed out again in rage and frustration and hurled himself at Groach, taking a springing leap into the air and driving the pommel of his sword into the beast's face with all of his might. Groach didn't cry out, or even stagger slightly – but he *did* drop Argon, who tumbled down among the rocks and clutched wildly at his throat.

Groach turned around slowly to catch Argon again, but his foot slipped on one of the rocks and, for the briefest of seconds, he was caught off balance.

Ruma took the initiative, and charged. The scrawny Etrurian would normally have bounced off Groach's bulbous stomach like a pebble ricocheting off a wall, but on this occasion the momentum was with him. He slammed into Groach with both knees extended. At the same time, Olu scrambled back over the rocks, crouching down behind Groach and bunching himself into a ball.

The monster crashed backwards and rolled over Olu and on to the steep incline. He managed to save himself from the ocean plunge by digging one of his massive hands into a rock crevice, his arm muscles barely showing the strain. As Ruma watched, however, Groach lost his footing and fell further. Above him, Olu was clutching at his face – evidently the beast's boot had caught the thin slave as he tumbled over. Still, although Olu was badly dazed, he was at least alive . . .

Ruma decided against pursuing Groach, and dashed off to help Decimus instead.

A short distance away, the young gladiator was now covered in savage cuts as the vultures continued to attack him. The two insane predators wheeled around in the air, and both lunged for his shoulders at the same moment. Decimus made a frantic

grab for his fallen sword, but was snatched off the ground and

carried –

struggling madly –

into the air.

Argon and Ruma

skidded to a halt beneath

their captured friend, and both

speedily dived after him. Ruma missed by

several inches and hit the rocks, hard, but

Argon caught hold of Decimus's right leg and

used all his weight to bring the young gladiator

back to ground. The vultures flew into a berserk and chaotic rage as Decimus was ripped from their claws and landed, bleeding profusely from the slashes on his shoulders, on the edge of the rock.

Thinking on his feet, Argon quickly snatched up a heavy-looking stone from the ground and took aim, firing it off at the vultures with all his strength. Ruma had thought of the same attack and was already back on the offensive, hurling rock after rock at the foul-smelling predators. The slaves both continued in this fashion while Decimus tried to examine the depth of his new wounds. To his amazement, they began to heal up before his eyes, forming scars that quickly disappeared back into his flesh as if they had never existed. He gasped, his mind momentarily shaken from the heat of the battle as he felt the White Snake's venom course through his veins.

Beside him, the battle against the vultures raged on.

A rain of missiles flew through the air in the direction of the birds. Most of them missed, but Argon's last shot caught one of the creatures square in the beak and it fell down, plummeting into the ocean with a satisfying splash. As Decimus reclaimed his sword from the ground, the second vulture came in for another swoop, this time with Ruma as its target. It screamed through the air, claws reaching out to destroy the scrawny Etrurian. Then, there was a strangled cry from the bird and a spray of blood showered the rock – Decimus had slashed directly through one of its wings. The giant predator hit the ground and flapped around madly with the remaining wing, rolling over on the rock several times before it finally toppled off the edge and plummeted into the ocean after its drowned companion.

Ruma let out a gasp of relief as both Decimus and Argon wiped the vulture's blood from their faces.

'Where are the others?' Decimus asked distractedly, his eyes searching among the rocks for Doom. There was no sign of the overlord, either.

'Gladius took off for the fort,' Ruma spluttered. 'I don't know why, but we sent Teo after hiiiiiiiiiii—'

A massive hand clamped on Ruma's shoulder and wrenched him into the air. As Decimus and

Argon looked on in stunned silence, Ruma flew backwards with lightning speed, soared through the rushing wind and skimmed over the rocks like a pebble. He slammed into Olu just as the thin slave finally struggled to his feet, and the pair collided, hard.

Groach growled with satisfaction and drove a punch into Argon's jaw which actually spun the Gaul in a somersault and laid him out on the ground, flat. In just a few seconds, the monster had taken down *three* of the slaves.

Decimus gripped his sword, and advanced. He knew that he had little hope of delivering a sword strike that was capable of penetrating this *thing*'s flesh, and he also knew that one punch from Groach would probably send him to Dreamland, but he had to try *something*.

The monster lunged forward, and Decimus
stepped aside, spinning his sword in the air and
bringing it round in a wild arc to slash a deep
wound in Groach's vein-riddled chest. At least,
that was the plan – unfortunately his blade was
clamped in mid-air by the monster's enormous

hands, ripped from his grasp and snapped in half like a twig.

Decimus took a leap back, and his eyes widened with horror. Not for the first time, he had trouble believing Groach was even human. Still, there was no choice but to fight him. No choice at all . . .

Gladius hurtled through the fort, opening every door he could find and frantically searching the rooms beyond, only to emerge from each one in a state of despair.

'What look for?' Teo managed, catching up with Gladius as he panted his way out of a dusty old storeroom.

Gladius pointed to the fort's outer defences. 'I'm trying to get up there,' he said, determinedly. 'Not the tower; I mean the lower wall; the battlements. I can't find the way, though – there's no stairs anywhere!'

Teo frowned. 'What there?'

'I saw something,' Gladius explained, hurrying off again towards another set of doors. 'Something that might help us. Quick! That weirdly-shaped door over there looks promising!'

Gladius dashed off again, leaving a bewildered Teo in his wake.

The new door, it turned out, led to a flight of steps that eventually arrived on the lower battlements. Gladius hared along the top of the wall and skidded to a halt beside what appeared to be a wooden framework of some sort.

Teo hurried up beside the big slave.

'What it is?' he asked.

Gladius put his head on one side, and studied
the object very carefully.

'I think it's a catapult,' he muttered,
crouching beside the

apparatus and examining it. 'Except, it doesn't use ropes to fling stuff into the air. It uses *this stuff*.' He pointed to a slimy green length of cord that ran from the two wooden struts. 'It looks almost like . . . well, snakeskin!'

Teo looked increasingly bewildered, but Gladius didn't wait for more questions. Instead, he snatched one side of the catapult and used all his weight to swing the frame around.

'You see that pile of stones over there, Teo? Bring them here! Now! Run!'

Gladius returned his attention to the snakeskin cord and, snatching up a handful, began to stretch it. Then he moved back, further and further, until it was stretched so tight that he could even hear the wood begin to creak and scream.

'It no work! It no work!' Teo shouted, hurrying

up to Gladius and wedging the stone inside the
skin.

'Hmm ...' said Gladius. 'We'll soon see.'

Decimus dodged every punch, kick, head-butt
and elbow-slam that Groach threw out. He used
every tiny reserve of his speed and his stealth to
outfight and outmanoeuvre the monster,
delivering several blows that he strongly
suspected would have had Doom's *last* apprentice,
Drin Hain, begging for mercy. Groach, however,
barely seemed *aware* of the attack. He simply
lunged after Decimus, taking every opportunity
to launch clumsy punches of his own that missed
by a mile.

Then it happened.

Decimus dived to his left, skipped over a kick that was intended to catch him on the rebound . . . and ran right into Groach's fist. The beast was evidently not quite as stupid as he'd thought.

It was only one punch, thrown at a strange angle with no particular effort behind it – but Decimus was caught completely off guard. The fist slammed into the side of the young gladiator's jaw, and knocked him out cold.

Groach grunted with satisfaction, and cracked his knuckles. One final, crushing blow and the insignificant whelp who had shamed his master would then be somebody else's problem . . .

On the ground, Decimus twitched slightly . . . but remained unconscious.

Groach padded over to stand beside the fallen

gladiator, and raised a foot over the boy's skull.

Suddenly, there was a rush of air and a barely audible crack. Groach staggered sideways, a spray of blood, flesh and bone flying out from the side of his head.

Then the big beast simply crashed to the ground and he didn't get up again.

A distant cry from Gladius signalled that the catapult was definitely working.

CHAPTER
IV

DOOMED

When Decimus awoke, Argon, Olu and Ruma were standing over him with concerned expressions on their faces. Before he managed to focus properly on any one of them, however, Teo and Gladius arrived.

'G-Groach is dead,' Decimus managed, weakly. 'S-something hi—'

'Yeah.' Gladius grimaced. 'I know – Teo and I got him with the catapult. He was about to crush your skull with his foot.'

The friends looked over at the fallen monster, and shuddered.

'So your snake-venom blood doesn't make you immune to being knocked out, then?' Ruma hazarded, as the others shared some puzzled looks.

Decimus shook his head. 'To be honest, I think

it might be wearing off – my jaw definitely hurts.'

'Mine too,' said Argon, illustrating his pain with a wince.

'What are we going to do about Doom?' Ruma muttered.

'Yeah, Doom!' added Olu. 'He took off over the rocks after summoning those vultures, and now he's in a rowing boat that's headed back towards his ship. Do you think he's actually scared?'

'You can bet he's scared,' Argon chimed in. 'In fact, when he finds out we've bested both his vultures *and* Groach, I reckon he'll flee completely.'

'NOT this time,' said Decimus, using his friends to help him get to his feet. 'This time, Doom isn't going anywhere.'

'So, what do we do?' Ruma asked, staring from

one of his companions to another. 'Swim after him?'

There was a chorus of half-amused laughter, but no hint of a smile appeared on Decimus's tired face.

'That's EXACTLY what we're going to do. We might not beat the rowing boat to the ship, but we'll certainly reach it before he has time to sail it away.'

Olu and Argon glanced at each other, but again it was the Etrurian who spoke.

'Are you serious?'

'I told you before, Ruma, we *NEED* to finish this. If Doom gets away again, he'll just set another trap for us in a year when we all think we're free of him. I don't expect any of you to come with me, but I'm going after him – *now*.'

Decimus steeled himself and slowly began to run towards the rocks. When he got to the edge of the cliff, he dived into the ocean below, sending up a long plume of spray.

There was a moment of grim silence … and then the others followed, even Gladius, who wasn't the strongest of swimmers and suspected that he wouldn't be able to reach the ship without a miracle.

The slaves dashed down the narrowest part of the rocky path, hitting the water at a dead run and carving their way through the ocean as if their lives depended on it.

The little rowing boat rose and fell on the ocean waves, as Doom scowled with annoyance at having to work the oars himself.

A short distance ahead of him, the other group

of soldiers were staring worriedly down from the ship and several were beginning to lower the rope ladders.

'Set sail!' the overlord screamed, glancing back towards Pin Yon Rock with rising fear. 'Set sail now!'

Silence signalled that the small crew couldn't quite hear their master above the roar of the waves.

Doom began to row faster, cursing under his breath. All the time, his mind was racing, plaguing him with a thousand thoughts. *The vultures were no longer visible in the air over the rock – could that mean the slaves had defeated them? And there was no sign of movement on the rock, either – surely Groach couldn't have been bested in combat? That beast was unstoppable; the merchants had sworn to it.*

A panic was rising in Doom's chest. At the

outset of his trap, he dreamed he would emerge

from China with the power to heal, an army of

golems at his side and the death of Decimus Rex

and his friends to celebrate. Now, the army lay in

ruins, the slaves might still be alive and Decimus himself had the power of the snake's venom. They had ruined his hard work once again!

So lost in his misery was Doom that he actually didn't realize he'd reached the ship until the edge of his rowing boat slammed into it. He almost lost his balance, and a single oar slipped from his grasp and splashed into the water.

'Are you OK, sir?' came a worried shout from the top of the ship, as Doom began to scramble up the swinging ladder.

'Stop talking and set sail NOW!' the overlord screamed at the top of his voice, clambering aboard and immediately taking hold of his war sergeant by the throat. 'Are you deaf? I told you to move this stinking SHIP!'

All five of the soldiers immediately hurtled

into their various positions, and several barked commands were issued and quickly obeyed. The ship slowly began to pull out of the harbour, and Doom breathed an audible sigh of relief. He grimaced as he surveyed the whole of Pin Yon Rock – there was still no sign of movement.

The ship was slowly beginning to move at a decent pace, when the overlord finally allowed himself a smile.

'Bring up the ladder, sergeant!' he shouted. 'We are away.'

'Yes, sir!' came the obedient reply. 'We are away, siiiiiiaargghh—'

The cry faded quickly, as the war sergeant was suddenly hauled over the side of the ship.

Argon appeared in his place, leaping on to the deck and immediately attacking the nearest soldier with a rain of well-aimed punches.

Two other guards abandoned their posts at one of the mainsails and hurried over to assist in the fight, but were intercepted by Ruma, Olu and Teo. In no time at all, a full-scale fight was in progress: screams echoed, sails were ripped apart and barrels were broken open. The slaves fought with a new determination. Teo high-kicked his way past two soldiers, Olu choked and strangled two more, Argon hurled three of the guards overboard and Ruma punched, elbowed and knee-dropped a further four all in quick succession. By the time Gladius puffed and panted his way over the port side of the ship, the battle was all but over. The slaves had made quick work of the guards.

Slavious Doom glared down at the assembled invaders, and scanned the deck for any sign of

Decimus Rex, but the young gladiator was
nowhere to be seen.

'So,' he boomed, drawing a sword so long that it
seemed to take a lifetime to remove the weapon
from its scabbard. 'I see your leader has fallen? A
shame – for all your skills in battle, my young
friends, I will make quick work of all of you.'

The overlord flashed a demonic smile and took
a single, giant step towards the lower deck ... but a
sudden familiar voice stopped him in his tracks.

'DOOM.'

Hesitating for a mere second, the overlord slowly turned to face his nemesis.

Decimus Rex, dripping wet and carrying a sword that looked as though it might fall apart at any second, glared up at him with total malice.

'You think you can fight me with *that*?' Doom mocked, glancing down at the ordinary-looking weapon in the boy's hands. 'My blade has been forged by the master-smiths of Rome – only one such blade is made by each in a lifetime.'

A smirk curled Decimus's cracked lips.

'It doesn't matter WHO made that sword, Doom, if there's still a coward holding it. Now do you actually *fight* without your men behind you, or are you merely – as I suspect – all talk? *We* want to find out, Doom – *ALL of us, together – the destroyers of all your precious plans.*'

Slavious Doom released his rage in a burst of energy that seemed to drive him forward like a cannonball. He slammed into Decimus Rex and knocked the boy backwards on to the lower deck. Then, leaping down from the roof of the captain's cabin, he hurtled towards the others.

Ruma was the first to snatch up a sword from one of the fallen soldiers. He hared across the deck and thrust the blade forward, just as Doom was about to strike down and finish Decimus off.

Ruma gritted his teeth and spittle began to drip from between his lips.

'You used me against my friends,' the Etrurian spat. 'Now you'll pay for that.'

Doom suddenly drove his own sword upwards, twisted Ruma's blade around and slammed his boot across it, breaking the weapon in half. Then he drove a fist into the scrawny Etrurian's jaw and sent him crashing to the deck.

'I'll be dead and buried before I'm bested by a sorrowful *traitor*,' he snapped.

He turned again and kicked Decimus in the stomach, rolling the young gladiator over as he tried to get up. Another kick knocked him unconscious.

'Now, boy, you will DIE.'

Again Doom's sword flew towards its intended victim, and again it was blocked by another blade.

Argon glared at the overlord with grim defiance.

'You'll find me harder to turn aside than Ruma,' he muttered. 'I have a little more STRENGTH to offer you.'

The Gaul whirled round and brought his blade through the air in a wild sweep. It clashed off

Doom's own sword, driving the overlord back several steps. However, when Argon raced in to take advantage of the move, the overlord twisted aside, tripping his opponent with a kick to the back of the knee and following it up with a lightning chop that caught the Gaul across the back of the neck.

Argon hit the deck, and Doom cackled evilly.

'What use is strength when there is no brain to guide it,' he spat.

When he returned his attention to Decimus, however, he found both Teo and Olu standing before him.

'Well,' Doom growled. 'What do we have here? If it isn't the weak links of the team! Who's first? The one who crept out of the arena like a rat in Decimus's shadow or the one who only draws *breath* because I saved his pathetic existence?'

Teo ran forward first, leaping into the air with a series of spinning kicks. Although none of them connected with Doom's face, the overlord was quickly sent staggering back to the cabin door. Three further kicks *did connect*, however, sending Doom crashing *through* the door and into the gloom within.

Teo somersaulted forward, leapt into the air once again – and was caught by the throat. Hulking himself up with a roar of anger, Doom tightened his free hand around the little slave's neck and propelled him backwards. Teo flew through the demolished door like a small dart, rolled over several times on the deck and collided with a barrel. The little slave tried to get up again, but collapsed with the effort.

'Fast, but weak,' Doom growled, twirling his

long sword as he emerged from the cabin and padded towards Olu. 'The tiny gnat *was* useful as bait for my trap, however.'

'You will never set another trap, Doom,' muttered Olu, stepping forward and raising a sword.

Doom let out a booming laugh.

'Slower than Teo, weaker than Argon and less cunning than Ruma. You might as well lower that weapon before you even *attempt* to strike.'

Olu screamed and ran directly into the overlord. Evidently, Doom hadn't been expecting such a straightforward attack and was alarmed by the sheer ferocity of Olu. Continuing to scream like a possessed lunatic, the skinny slave stormed forward in a tornado of sword strikes. The clash of steel was deafening as Doom found he needed to block thrust after thrust after thrust. The last strike was so powerful that Olu actually embedded the sword in the wall of the cabin. Doom immediately seized upon the precious second it took Olu to remove the blade, and lunged at him. Driving a calculated punch at the skinny slave's head, Doom swiftly blasted Olu sideways. Then he spun the sword around and drove the hilt up into the boy's face, opening a vicious cut across his jaw and flooring him at the same time.

'Surprising,' Doom admitted, stepping over the fallen slave. 'But all energy and no skill leaves you lacking in the presence of one so great as *me*.'

The overlord marched into the centre of the deck, and smiled at the scene before him.

Decimus was awake once again, helped on to his feet by Gladius, who stayed at his side until he was steady. Both of them were looking upon Doom with ill-concealed hatred.

'And so it comes to this . . .' Doom smiled, raising his sword with both hands. 'The first two names I scrawled on my list become the last two slaves to stand against me. How amusing – the unsung hero of Arena Primus and his rather large friend.'

Decimus snatched up his sword and rushed forward, but as Doom prepared to block the assault he suddenly veered aside at the last second and leapt away from him.

The overlord

spotted

the trap too late, and spun around. Gladius crashed into him like a battering ram, sending the great sword flying into the ocean as Doom hit the deck with a thunderous crash.

'The great thing about being large...' Gladius mumbled, driving a boot into the overlord's face, '...is that it doesn't really matter how tall and scary your opponent is – if you run into them hard enough, they go down.'

Gladius reached down and snatched hold of Doom, dragging him to his feet. As the overlord was hauled up, however, he thrust an open hand at Gladius's throat, jabbing him sharply. Gladius coughed and spluttered as Doom scrambled on the deck for a replacement sword. He'd only just found one and made it on to his feet when Decimus finally made his move. The young gladiator raced forward, slamming his sword against Doom's newly acquired blade. Steel met steel, and then the overlord dropped on to his stomach, sweeping the young gladiator's legs out from under him.

As Decimus went down, Doom quickly regained his footing and rolled on to his knees, just in time to parry a new assault from Gladius. Blocking Gladius's attack successfully, Doom threw the replacement sword aside and snatched hold of the slave's weakened neck with both hands. Conscious that he had only a few vital seconds before Decimus would be upon him, Doom charged forward with all his might, driving his captive back against the cabin wall. Gladius's neck was so thick that Doom quickly found himself unable to close his grip around the flesh completely. He was doubly surprised, when Gladius brought both arms up in a mighty blast which actually broke the hold wide open. Doom took his only remaining opportunity, and slammed his head forward, his skull glancing off Gladius's own in one mad crunch.

Gladius crumpled to the ground, moaned a few times and then passed out.

Doom spun around, expecting the long-delayed thrust of a sword from Decimus Rex. In fact, the young gladiator no longer held a weapon. Instead, he threw the hardest punch Doom had ever taken in his life. Decimus's fist ricocheted off the overlord's jaw, but the blow was enough to send the big man staggering sideways.

'I've wanted to do that since the first day I saw you,' Decimus muttered, lunging forward with two more stomach punches and a knee-lift that sent Doom crashing on to his back. 'When you take people from their homes, and their families ... you have to expect, just once in a while, that some of them ... will ... fight ... back.'

Decimus suddenly exploded in a frenzy that made Olu's attack seem tame. He charged forward, dragging the overlord along the deck and kicking him repeatedly. Then, hauling him on to his feet once again, Decimus pushed him against the starboard side of the ship and slapped him across the face.

'Is this it?' Decimus screamed, his voice now edged with every emotion wrestling for control of his soul. 'Is this ALL you've got, when it comes right down to it?'

Doom surged forward with an almighty bellow

of rage and threw a wild punch.

Decimus stepped aside and slammed a fist into his jaw.

'Is this the great Slavious Doom without all his plans and his cronies? A pathetic . . .'

The overlord kicked out this time, but Decimus caught his leg, spun him around and punched him twice as hard as before.

'. . . feeble . . .'

Doom tried the trusted head-butt that had taken care of Gladius, but he missed by a long way. Decimus drove his elbow into Doom's chest.

'. . . *useless* . . .'

The overlord staggered back against the side of the ship.

'. . . sack of bones.'

With one last roar of triumph, Decimus Rex

charged forward. He careered into Slavious Doom with both arms extended sending the dishevelled, defeated warrior over the side of the ship.

'Arggghghghhhhhhhhhhhhhhhhhhhhhhhh!'

There was a distant splash and, all at once, the great overlord of Arena Primus was no more.

Decimus dropped to his knees and spewed a mixture of saliva and seawater on to the deck. His exhaustion was only matched by his sense of relief, and he quickly felt all his energy draining out of him. His limbs seemed to buckle, but just as he was about to collapse completely, an arm took hold of his shoulder.

Decimus looked up into the eyes of Gladius, who smiled through several broken teeth. He was about to speak out when another hand closed on his arm, followed by another, and another. Ruma,

Olu, Argon and Teo all helped Gladius to get

their incredible, heroic friend to his feet.

'Doom,' Decimus managed. 'He's . . .

'Gone,' Gladius finished. 'We

know. You did it: you finally

defeated him!'

The young gladiator shook

his head.

'We did it,' he corrected him.

'All of us – we did it together.'

The slaves made their way across

the deck, some staggering, some

bleeding, all of them tired and weary

from their many adventures.

'Does anybody know how we

actually sail home from this place?'

Ruma hazarded. 'Or what

actual direction it is we're supposed to be going in?'

Olu, Teo and Argon all looked at each other blankly. Even Gladius could only offer a reluctant shrug.

'We'll find a way home,' Decimus said, allowing himself to smile for the first time since he'd discovered that Teo was still alive. 'We always find a way.'

GLADIATOR GAME
WAR!

This game pits Slavious Doom, Groach, the giant vultures and the guards against Decimus, Ruma, Olu, Argon, Teo, Gladius and the golem army. But it's not quite as simple as that! How good a general would you be if you only had a limited amount of money to spend? Here you can find out!

Each player tosses a coin and chooses a side. From there, it's like picking a football team – each player starts with 30 points and can pick their team. Of course, you can only select from your OWN side! Choose wisely!

Argon (5 pts)

Decimus (10 pts)

Gladius (5 pts)

Olu (5 pts) Teo (5 pts) Ruma (5 pts)

Golems
(3 pts each)

Slavious
Doom (10pts)

Groach (20pts)

Giant Vulture (3pts)

Guards
(1pt each)

Giant Vulture (3pts)

Each character has the following number of lives:

THE SLAVE ARMY:
Golems (2L each),
Decimus (5L),
Ruma, Olu, Gladius, Argon, Teo (3L each).

THE DOOM ARMY:
Guards (1L each),
Slavious Doom (4L),
Groach (5L),
Giant Vulture (2L each).

Each player now chooses one of their army characters to fight and they take it in turns to close their eyes and stab a pencil into the grid. The results in the grid tell you how many lives each character has lost. The first number represents the Slave Army, the second represents the Roman Army.
Example: player one selects Ruma to fight and

player two selects a Giant Vulture. Player one then jabs a pencil into the grid with his/her eyes closed and sees that he has struck a 2/1 grid. Therefore, Ruma (who has 5 life points) loses 2 life points and is left with 3. The Giant Vulture (who has 3 life points) loses 1 life point and is left with 2. If Ruma had lost 5 life points, he would have been defeated. For the Giant Vulture, 3 life points would have removed it from the game. Now play on!

0/0	0/0	0/0	0/0	0/0	0/0	0/0	0/0	0/0
0/0	1/0	0/1	1/0	2/1	1/2	0/1	1/0	2/1
1/0	0/1	1/0	5/4	1/2	2/1	1/0	0/1	1/2
0/1	1/0	0/1	1/0	2/1	1/2	0/1	1/0	5/4
1/0	0/1	1/0	0/1	1/2	2/1	1/0	0/1	1/2
0/1	1/0	0/1	1/0	2/1	1/2	0/1	1/0	2/1
1/0	0/1	1/0	0/1	1/2	2/1	1/0	0/1	1/2
0/1	1/0	0/1	1/0	2/1	1/2	0/1	1/0	2/1
1/0	0/1	1/0	4/5	3/1	1/3	1/0	0/1	4/5
0/1	1/0	0/1	1/0	1/3	3/1	0/1	1/0	1/3
0/0	0/0	0/0	0/0	0/0	0/0	0/0	0/0	0/0

0/0	1/2	2/1	1/2	2/1	1/2	2/1	1/2	1/3	3/1	0/0
0/0	2/1	1/2	2/1	1/2	2/1	1/2	2/1	3/1	1/3	0/0
0/0	1/2	2/1	1/2	2/1	1/2	2/1	1/2	1/3	3/1	0/0
0/0	2/1	1/2	2/1	1/2	2/1	1/2	2/1	3/1	1/3	0/0
0/0	1/2	2/1	1/2	2/1	1/2	2/1	1/2	1/3	3/1	0/0
0/0	1/0	5/4	1/0	0/1	1/0	0/1	1/0	4/5	1/0	0/0
0/0	2/1	1/2	2/1	1/2	2/1	1/2	2/1	3/1	1/3	0/0
0/0	1/2	2/1	1/2	2/1	1/2	2/1	1/2	1/3	3/1	0/0
0/0	0/1	1/0	0/1	1/0	0/1	1/0	0/1	1/0	0/1	0/0

CHARACTER PROFILE
GOLEMS

NAME: Golems (race name)

FROM: Pin Yon Rock, South China Sea

HEIGHT: 1.83 metres

BODY TYPE: Clay; cracked, animated

Fact File:

Difficult to defeat in combat, though they can be smashed.

Many years ago, they were enslaved and frozen by the arrival of a demonic reptile known as the White Snake.

Once awakened they can be commanded by the conscious thoughts of the White Snake's slayer.

GOLEM QUIZ: How well do you know the Golem Army? Can you answer the following three questions?

1. WHAT COLOUR IS THE WHITE SNAKE'S POISON?

2. WHO DESTROYS A GOLEM WITH ONE PUNCH?

3. WHO IS THE FIRST PERSON TO HEAR THE GOLEMS' THOUGHTS?

Answers: 1. Green p.14 2. Groach p.41 3. Ruma p.17

HOW MANY OF

GLADIATOR BOY

SERIES TWO HAVE YOU COLLECTED?

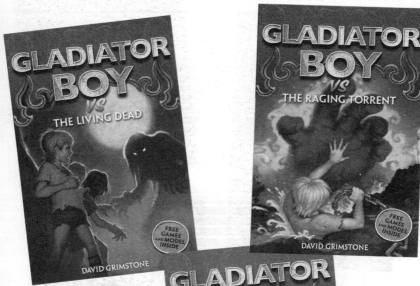

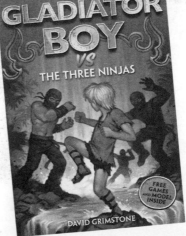

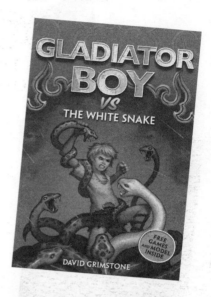

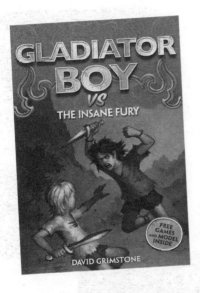

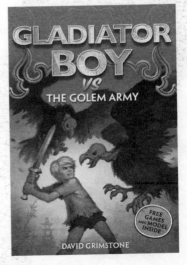

GLADIATOR BOY

WWW.GLADIATORBOY.COM

Have you checked out the Gladiator Boy website? It's the place to go for games, downloads, activities, sneak previews and lots of fun!

Sign up to the newsletter at **WWW.GLADIATORBOY.COM** and receive exclusive extra content and the opportunity to enter special members-only competitions.

GLADIATOR BOY

CAN'T WAIT UNTIL THE NEXT GLADIATOR BOY COMES OUT?

DESPERATE TO KNOW WHAT HAPPENS NEXT?

Find out now on
WWW.GLADIATORBOY.COM
with an exclusive online story from
David Grimstone!